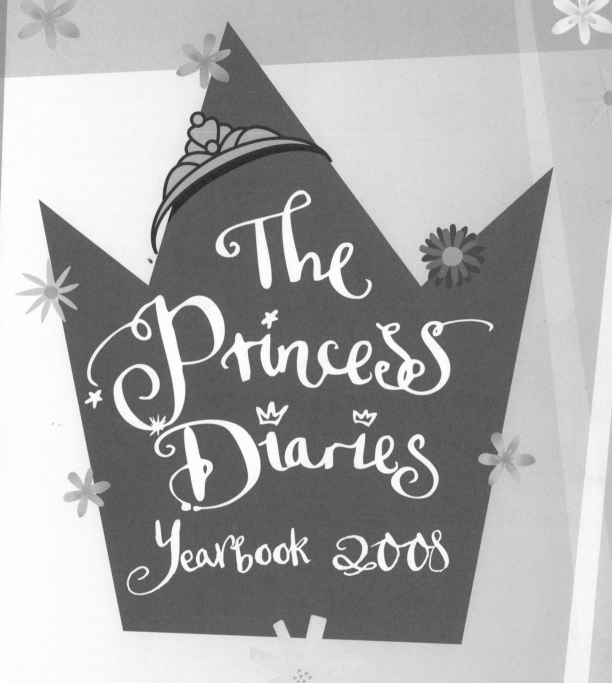

The Princess Diaries

Yearbook 2008

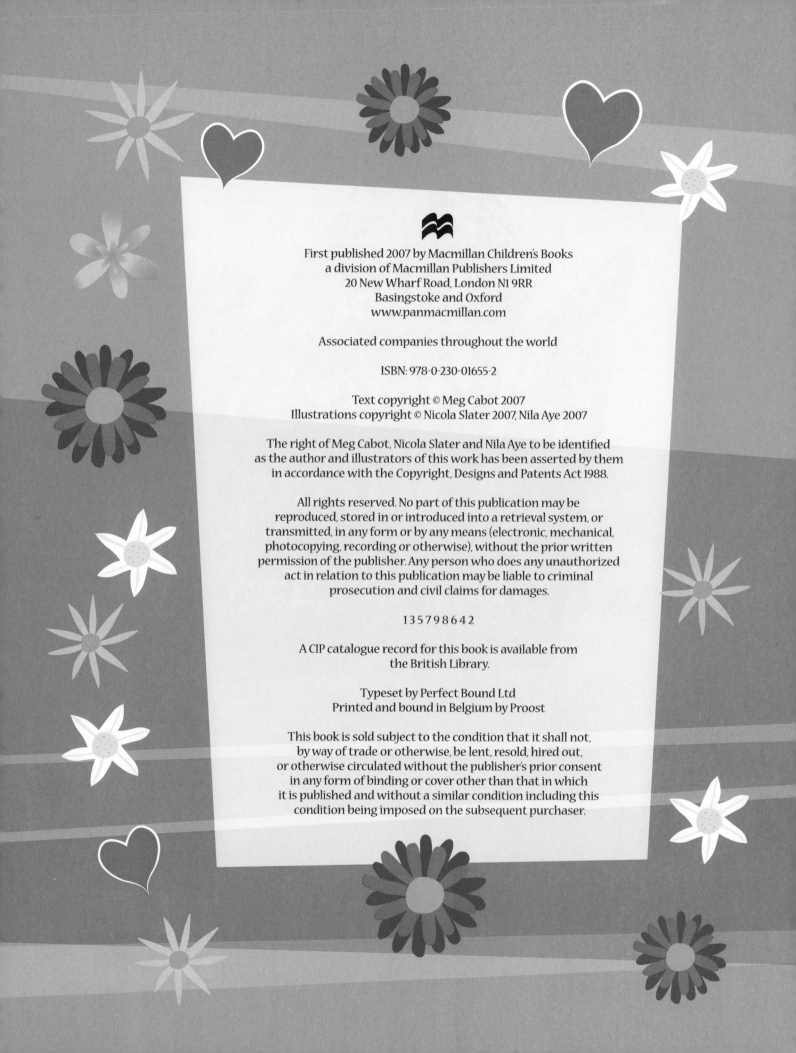

First published 2007 by Macmillan Children's Books
a division of Macmillan Publishers Limited
20 New Wharf Road, London N1 9RR
Basingstoke and Oxford
www.panmacmillan.com

Associated companies throughout the world

ISBN: 978-0-230-01655-2

A CIP catalogue record for this book is available from
the British Library.

Typeset by Perfect Bound Ltd
Printed and bound in Belgium by Proost

The Princess Diaries

Yearbook 2008

MEG CABOT

MACMILLAN

Contents

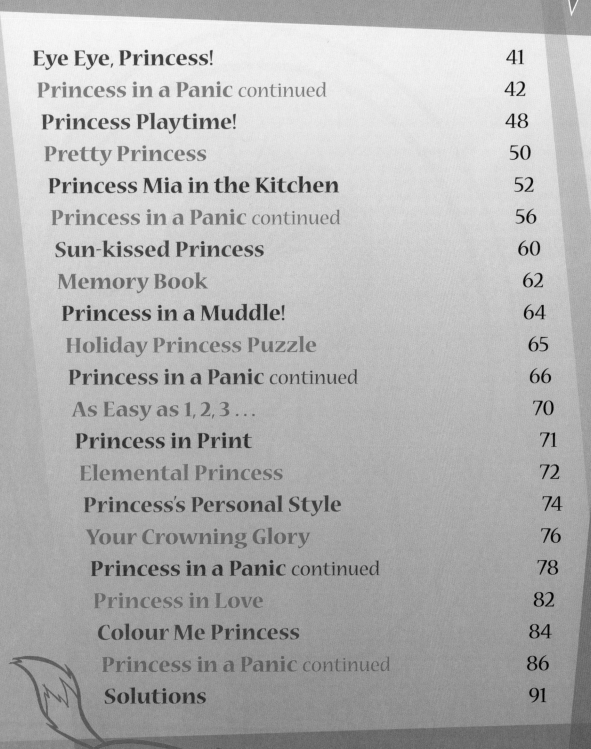

HEY, PRINCESS!

Welcome to my second Yearbook!
Has a whole year really passed already?!

I just know your 2008 is going to be crammed
with all kinds of princessy fun and fabulousness.

So here's to a new year —
and to every princess on the planet!

Lots of love,

Mia
xx

**Amelia Mignonette Grimaldi Thermopolis Renaldo
Princess of Genovia**

My New Year's Resolutions for 2008

I will improve myself in the following ways:

1. Math
2. Singing +acting
3. Dancing

I will break the following unprincessy habits:

1. Talking with food in my mouth.
2. Chewing with my mouth open.
3. ~~Spitting!~~ Not using manners

I will not be too tough on myself for failing to uphold the above resolutions. Instead I will:

1. Think of all the great things I can do.
2. Look in the mirror and say "This girl is a princess"
3. Put on my tiara and know that I am a princess!

Princess Wishes

You can wish for all kinds of things: happiness for yourself and your friends, good school grades, money, love. You have to work hard to make your wishes and dreams come true – but anything is possible . . .

The perfect moments for making your wishes come true:

 Blowing out a candle

 Seeing a shooting star

 Breaking a wishbone

 Throwing a coin in a fountain

 When you see a white horse

 Blowing an eyelash off your fingertip

 When you say the same words at the same time as someone else

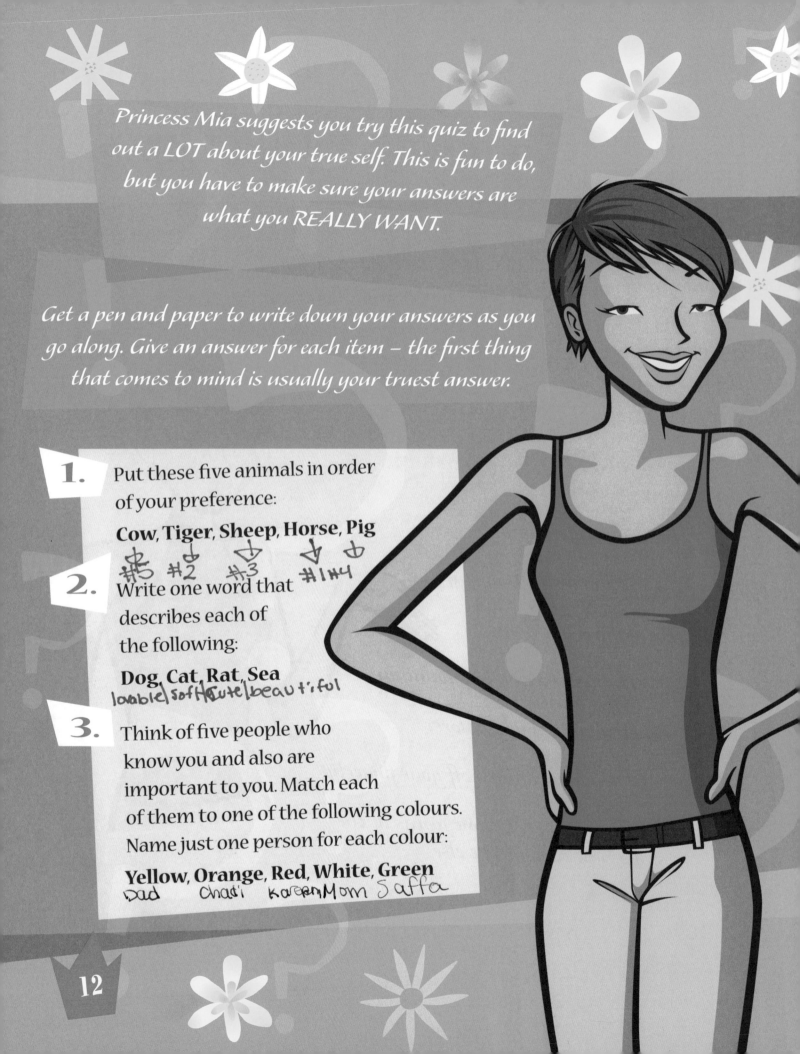

Princess Mia suggests you try this quiz to find out a LOT about your true self. This is fun to do, but you have to make sure your answers are what you REALLY WANT.

Get a pen and paper to write down your answers as you go along. Give an answer for each item – the first thing that comes to mind is usually your truest answer.

1. Put these five animals in order of your preference:

Cow, Tiger, Sheep, Horse, Pig

#5   #2   #3   #1 #4

2. Write one word that describes each of the following:

Dog, Cat, Rat, Sea

lovable/soft/cute/beautiful

3. Think of five people who know you and also are important to you. Match each of them to one of the following colours. Name just one person for each colour:

Yellow, Orange, Red, White, Green

Dad   Chadi   Karen Mom   Saffa

Quiz for Life!

ANSWER KEY

1. This will define your priorities in your life.

Cow signifies CAREER
Tiger signifies PRIDE
Sheep signifies LOVE
Horse signifies FAMILY
Pig signifies MONEY

2. Your description of the **dog** describes your own personality.
Your description of the **cat** describes the personality of your boyfriend – or future boyfriend!
Your description of the **rat** describes the personality of your enemies.
Your description of the **sea** describes your own life.

3. **Yellow:** someone you will never forget
Orange: someone you consider your true friend
Red: someone that you really love
White: your twin soul
Green: someone that you will remember for the rest of your life

13

Princess Boudoir

A princess's boudoir is the centre of her kingdom. Here are some top tips for making your bedroom the coolest in the realm.

Keep it tidy – you and your friends will actually want to spend time in your boudoir if there aren't piles of junk everywhere!

Chill-out zone – beanbags and fluffy rugs provide great extra seating for when fellow princesses come round. Keep a well-stocked magazine rack nearby so you can flick through mags together while listening to your favourite tunes.

14

Dressing table – use pretty boxes and baskets to keep your stuff organized. Keep a framed photo of you and your best friend looking fabulous to inspire you when you're getting ready!

Get creative – posters, pictures, photos, lighting, flowers can all express your personal style.

Decorate – try painting one wall a striking colour, or hanging some funky patterned wallpaper to make a statement. New curtains or blinds make a big difference too.

Plan out your new boudoir layout on this grid. Don't forget to leave room for your throne!

Princess Puzzle

The answers to these The Princess Diaries questions are hidden in the grid below. The words can be found horizontally and vertically and run backwards and forwards!

1. What kind of novels does Tina Hakim Baba like to read? *ROMANCES*

2. What instrument does Boris Pelkowski play? *VIOLIN*

3. Who gives Mia princess lessons? *GRAND MERE*

4. What is the name of Princess Mia's bodyguard? *LARS*

5. Frank Gianini is Mia's stepfather but he's also her teacher. Which subject does he teach? *ALGEBRA*

6. What is Mia's baby brother called? *ROCKY*

W	R	O	C	K	Y	N	B	Y	F	D	A
U	V	E	C	H	Y	N	S	W	P	K	L
G	R	A	N	D	M	E	R	E	O	D	G
H	W	B	I	Y	S	K	M	Q	L	Y	E
E	B	A	L	I	Q	B	A	M	X	N	B
A	U	Y	O	S	E	C	N	A	M	O	R
G	Y	S	I	L	A	R	S	Z	R	I	A
K	E	D	V	M	T	P	L	M	Q	X	S

(Answers are on page 91 in case you get stuck!)

Bring Out Your Inner Princess!

There is a lot more to being a princess than wearing a tiara and knowing which fork to use.

Just because you are kind, doesn't mean you have to be a pushover. It is princesslike to be assertive; it is unprincesslike to be walked all over.

Smile! Princesses always put their best face forward for the good of the kingdom's morale.

Random acts of kindness rock! Instant Messaging someone who seems down; offering to go to the movies with the new girl no one likes – these are extremely princessy things to do.

Be yourself. Being a princess is more of an attitude, really, than a way of life. And you know, even though there aren't enough countries on the planet for each of us to get a chance to reign supreme, it's possible for all of us to act like a princess!

Princess in a Panic

Uh-oh. Princess Mia has lost her precious diary . . .

Find out more in this hilarious THE PRINCESS DIARIES story.

Tuesday, October 25, 3 p.m., limo on the way to princess lessons

OK, so I'm dead. I know I say that a lot, but this time it's really true. This is bad. Not bad like the time I accidentally insulted the Sultan of Brunei by asking him if he ever gets his different wives confused, either. I'm talking *really* bad.

I lost my journal.

I know! The journal into which I pour my deepest innermost thoughts and feelings!

The journal which has helped me through some of my darkest hours and most socially precarious moments!

The journal in which I have recorded every single solitary thing that has ever happened to me, and almost every single thought I have ever had . . . including all those ones about how much I enjoy the smell of my boyfriend's neck!

And it's gone. Just gone.

Do you see why I'm so dead now?

I seriously thought it was just in my bodyguard Lars's gun case, because I had him put it there that time Lilly and J.P. and Tina and Boris and Michael and I all went bowling at Chelsea Piers the other night.

And I sort of forgot to ask for it back, on account of my princess lessons and midterms and Michael – you know, all the curtsying and studying and kissing I was doing. I mean, I barely had time to *breathe*, let alone write in my journal.

But today, when I finally had a minute to myself, I started looking around for it . . .

And I couldn't find it.

Princess in a Panic *continues on page 28*

The Power of Five!

For each category, record your personal top five.

MY TOP FIVE CELEBRITY ROYAL CONSORTS
(five celebs you'd love to hang out with)

1. Selena Gomez

2. Ariana Grande

3. Taylor Lautner

4. Lily Collins

5. ~~Justin Bieber~~

MY TOP FIVE NON-CELEBRITY ROYAL CONSORTS
(your five best friends!)

1. Saffa Mohamed

2. ~~Bri Korcy~~ Koshi

3. ~~Julia~~ Aepli

4. Katie Dunn

5. Katy Rudy

6. Althea Read

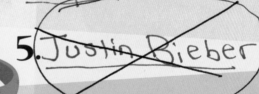

FIVE HOTTIES I WOULD DANCE WITH AT THE BALL

1.

2.

3.

4.

5.

TOP FIVE LAWS I'D PASS IF I REALLY RULED

1. Respect Me

2. No Home work

3. Every one earn [free] money

4.

5.

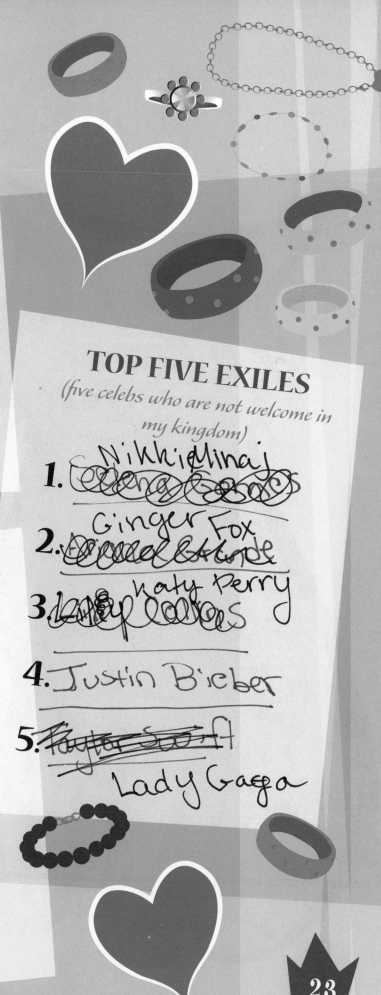

TOP FIVE EXILES
(five celebs who are not welcome in my kingdom)

1. ~~Nikki Minaj~~

2. ~~Ginger Fox~~

3. ~~Katy Perry~~

4. Justin Bieber

5. ~~Taylor Swift~~

Lady Gaga

23

Crazy About Cats

Fat Louie, Princess Mia's cat, is one much-loved kitty! Cats make great pets, but remember: they need a lot of looking after. Follow these tips and your cat will be as happy as Fat Louie!

Buying ready-prepared food ensures your cat has a balanced diet. Make sure your cat:

- **can always get to water**
- **doesn't eat food that contains caffeine or sugar.**

Most cats love to doze – make sure your cat has a quiet place to rest his little fluffy head.

Your cat needs a yearly check-up with a vet. The vet will be able to make sure your kitty stays healthy!

A healthy cat will groom itself regularly, but brushing your cat will:

- keep its coat looking healthy
- help you notice if it has fleas
- help reduce hairballs (hair that cats swallow when they groom themselves).

It's nice for your cat to go in and out as it likes, and having a cat flap makes life easier. It's a good idea to:

- keep a new cat indoors for a couple of weeks
- microchip your cat in case it gets lost.

It's important to house-train your cat so it doesn't make a mess indoors. Be patient and calm when training and try to:

- train your cat to go to the toilet in a litter tray or outside when it is young
- encourage your cat to use a scratching post instead of the furniture.

Lost Louie!

Fat Louie and Mia have been separated! This will not do! Can you help Fat Louie find his princess?

Turn to page 91 if you get lost.

Spot the Difference

At first glance, these two Princess Mias look exactly the same, but there are five differences to spot.

You can check your answers on page 91.

Princess in a Panic

continued from page 21

I tell you, I practically tore my room apart searching. Poor Fat Louie tried to hide under the bed to escape all the wadded-up pairs of underwear and orange peels that were flying around (I really need to clean my room one of these days).

Only Fat Louie's too fat to fit under the bed any more, so it was very traumatic for him. He could only get his head and shoulders under the bed. The rest of him – his tail and his big round butt – were sticking out from under the bed, quivering.

I had to give him a bunch of chicken-flavoured Pounce just to calm him down. Unlike me, Fat Louie is not a vegetarian, despite my many attempts to convert him.

It was while I was feeding Fat Louie that I remembered giving my journal to Lars the night we all went bowling. So I called him up, over at the suite in the Plaza he's sharing with my dad's bodyguard and our driver, and asked him for it.

And then Lars said the words that sent cold tentacles of fear creeping around my heart, just like they always talk about in books.

'Journal? I do not have your journal, Your Highness.'

I told him he was wrong. I said, 'No, really, Lars. Remember? I gave it to you the other night at Chelsea Piers. You even moved your Uzi clip over to make room for it.'

And even though Lars says he remembers doing that, my journal isn't in his gun case now.

Which means it could be anywhere. Really. ANYWHERE.

I'm dead. So dead.

When I think about all the people who could

find my private journal and read it and see things that might make them a) hate me, b) laugh at me or, worse, c) think that I might actually like them when I *don't*, I FREAK out. Seriously. I mean, I have poured the most closely kept, confidential secrets of my heart into that journal. Everything.

And I mean EVERYTHING.

And now it's gone. It's in the hands of someone who is probably reading it, most likely with great amusement, and possibly even derision. My private confessions are causing someone out there untold mirth.

Princess in a Panic *continues on page 42*

31

Princess Mia *ALWAYS* has something to say.

Why not copy down your favourite quote in your diary and use it as a source of inspiration this year?

You can always flick through your *The Princess Diaries* collection and pick out other characters' words of wisdom too.

'Remember, being a princess is all about being yourself.'

'There's one thing that looks good on everyone: confidence. Have confidence in yourself and your looks, and others will see the outer beauty as well as the inner. That's what everybody keeps telling me anyway . . .'

Say It Like It Is, Princess!

'All I can say is: be careful what you wish for. It might just come true.'

'For now I'll settle for what I've got. Because it's actually quite a lot, now that I come to think about it.'

'As a princess, I will always value princesslike qualities in other people, such as honesty and self-respect.'

'Not a single one of us is better than any other person here. And that includes any princesses that might be in the room.'

'Now go rule!'

Customizing Cool!

Follow these simple instructions to make a T-shirt that oozes cheerleader-chic . . .

- Choose a T-shirt – ideally one with a sporty/retro vibe but even plain white will look cool!

- Cut the neck of the T-shirt into a scoop.

- Take some scissors and snip the arms into strips.

- Grab some ribbon (any colour you like!) and tie to the top of the arm strips.

- You're good to go!

More customizing ideas

Make like a magpie and collect buttons, ribbons, sequins – anything colourful and shiny! When you're feeling creative, open up your box of customizing goodies, grab some fabric glue and discover your inner fashion designer!

Simply the Best

It's simple: just grab a pen and fill in the gaps! If your best friend has a go too you can compare lists. Then try again in a few months' time and see if your tastes have changed!

MY FAVOURITE . . .

Actor Johny Depp

Actress Selena Gomez

Singer Ariana Grande +Selena Gomez

Band One Direction

Song Give Your Heart a Break BY: Demi Lovato

Shop Mall - ABERCROMBIE

Item of clothing A lot - Nize but not too nice something

Chocolate Reses Peanut Butter Cups !!!!!! + Peanut Butter

Boy

Colour Neon Colours

35

Secret Shames!

Princess Mia has had her fair share of CRINGY moments. Grab a pen and write your silliest, funniest secrets on the wall of shame!

Ask your friends to add their most EMBARRASSING secrets too – and share the shame!

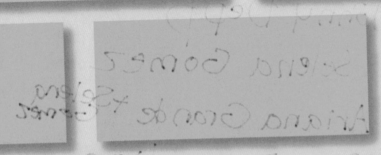

37

What's Your Style, Princess?

1. Who do you think is the most stylish?
a) Keira Knightley
b) Tess Daly
c) Fearne Cotton

2. What's your idea of a perfect Saturday afternoon?
a) Having a friend round to make and customize things
b) Preparing to party!
c) Shopping!

3. What's your favourite flavour lip balm?
a) Anything fruity
b) Vanilla
c) Mint

4. What's your favourite footwear?
a) Flip-flops in the summer and Uggs in the winter
b) Heels or funky pumps depending on what you're doing!
c) Trainers!

5. Which singer do you prefer?
a) Corinne Bailey Rae
b) Amy Winehouse
c) Lily Allen

If you picked mostly **A**, you're a HIPPY CHICK.

- Try wearing your hair down with lots of cute little plaits.
- You'll love beauty products that contain essential oils like lavender, rose and orange.
- Hunt down markets where you and your hippy-chick friends can find funky one-offs and vintage treasures.

If you picked mostly **B**, you're a GLAM GIRL.

- Try waving your hair and pinning with sparkly clips.
- Have a couple of friends round for a manicure session. Stock up on nail varnish – and don't forget your toes!
- There are loads of amazing dry-oil sprays in the shops that'll make your skin shimmer and shine – perfect for parties.

If you picked mostly **C**, you're a COOL CAT.

- How long has it been since you wore your hair in bunches – it'll look cute on you: try it!
- Experiment with hair mascara. Try colouring a small section of your hair a vibrant pink!
- Mix tomboyish T-shirts and trainers with funky jewellery and pretty make-up for a cool and quirky look.

Princess Puzzler

Grab a friend, two pens and two pieces of paper. Now each see how many different words you can make, using only letters from the words:

BEST PRINCESS FRIENDS

How did you do?

1–9 You're a pretty good team!

10–20 You're a top two!

21+ You're a perfect pair of princesses!

Eye Eye, Princess!

I bet you didn't know that the colour of your eyes can give some amazing insights into your personality . . .

DEEP BLUE - Gentle, sensitive, a good listener

LIGHT BLUE - Flirty, funny, strong

GREEN - Imaginative, creative, daring

GREY - Clever, thoughtful, romantic

BROWN - Warm, genuine, reliable

HAZEL - Keen on surprises, intriguing, friendly

Princess in a Panic

continued from page 31

I'm telling you, a person could go crazy just thinking about something like that.

So I did the only thing I could think of, in order to spare myself going insane: I called my dad right away in *his* suite at the Plaza, which of course he isn't sharing with anybody.

Anyway, I was all, 'Dad, this is really important. In fact, it could very well be a matter of total national security.'

Then I suggested he deploy some spies right away to get my journal back.

I'll tell you something about my father: he may be sovereign ruler of a small European country and all that, touted by many as being one of the most forward-thinking monarchs in Genovian history, thanks in no small part to the business-administration degree he earned here in the States when he was young.

But he has really got to do some work on his interpersonal relationships, because he is way unsympathetic to the plight of the post-millennial teen.

Besides, what kind of country doesn't have spies? I mean, I once saw on the news something about a spy from Luxembourg and I swear to God only about five people live in Luxembourg. Yet *they* have spies and Genovia doesn't. Does that make any sense? I mean, any sense at all?

I am telling you, the first thing I'm going to do after I take over the throne – once I've converted

the palace into a home for people's abandoned pets – is hire some spies.

So I suggested very nicely to my dad that maybe the Royal Genovian Air Force could be put on alert about it – you know, my missing journal – since I know that although Genovia may not have spies, we at least have a couple of jets, but my dad was like, 'Mia, have you lost your mind?'

The problem with my dad is that he doesn't go to the movies enough. If he did, then he would have seen that thing with Tom Cruise where it totally showed that there are like satellites up in

space that can detect things like people's missing microchips and journals and stuff.

Plus he would know that all anyone would have to do to get my lost journal back is don a Ninja outfit and lower himself by a cable through the skylight of the safe house in which it is being held.

So then I had no choice but to inform my dad that it was highly likely my journal has fallen into the hands of enemies of Genovia, who might use it in nefarious ways to bring down the House of Renaldo, which has ruled over our small

principality peacefully for nearly a millennium.

Or – even WORSE – that it might have fallen into the hands of some paparazzo, who intends to publish it in a newspaper as a serial.

Hey. You never know. It could happen!

But Dad totally doesn't believe me! I mean, about my journal having possibly fallen into the hands of Genovian enemies or the paparazzi!

Princess in a Panic continues on page 56

Princess Playtime!

At princess sleepovers and parties it's great to have some games up your sleeve. Try these:

THE NAME GAME

1. Give each person a Post-it note and a pen.

2. Get each person to write the name of a famous person on the paper.

3. Without letting them see the name you've written, stick the paper on the forehead of the friend next to you.

4. Each person has to guess who they are by asking the other players questions. The questions can only have a 'yes' or 'no' answer. They have twenty questions to get it right!

BIRTHDAY BANQUET!

Players sit in a circle. The first player starts by saying, 'At my birthday banquet I'd like to eat hamburgers.' The next player must repeat, 'At my birthday banquet I'd like to eat hamburgers and . . .(player adds another dish).' The game continues around the circle, with each player reciting the dishes in the correct order and then adding a new one. If a player makes a mistake they have to leave the circle and the game continues. The person left who can perfectly recite the birthday banquet menu wins!

After this game you'll probably be ready to eat.

PASS THE PARCEL

Yup, bet you haven't played this for a while. It's such fun though – give it a go! Before the party, wrap up the prize (what about a lipgloss, a pair of earrings, a photo frame, some choccies . . .) then take charge of starting and stopping the music while the others play. You can also ask your friends to each bring a small gift so that you can play more than once!

Pretty Princess

1. TWEEZER-HAPPINESS: Don't make the mistake of over-tweezing. Only pluck hairs from underneath your brows.

2. FOUNDATION O-D: Too much foundation makes you look like you're wearing a mask – SO not a good look. Most princesses only need to use a tinted moisturizer – and remember to blend well.

3. ZIT-PICKING: Picking spots before they're ready makes them worse. If you are going to squeeze, make sure your fingers are super-clean, apply gentle pressure and dab with tea-tree oil afterwards.

4. MASCARA MADNESS: Lots of mascara can look gorgeous for a big night out, but spider-leg lashes are a bad thing. Use a lash comb to separate if your mascara clumps.

5. MAKE-UP TO BED: Always take all your make-up off before you go to sleep. It only takes a couple of minutes . . .

6. LIP-SLICK: Too much dark lipstick makes your mouth look tiny. Much better to keep lips fresh and natural – gloss is a good bet.

7. PRODUCT OVERLOAD: Easy on the serum, hairspray, wax and mousse. Too much makes your hair look either dull or greasy. Build it up slowly – you need a lot less product than you think.

51

Princess Mia in the Kitchen

Here are a few of Princess Mia's favourite yummy treats, perfect for munching on at sleepovers, feeding to your family, devouring when alone . . .

Royal Chocolate Muffins
The chocolatiest muffins . . . ever.
(Makes 12)

250g plain flour
150g chocolate chips (plus extra for sprinkling)
2 teaspoons baking powder
½ teaspoon bicarbonate of soda
2 tablespoons cocoa
175g caster sugar
250ml milk
90ml vegetable oil
1 large egg

- Preheat the oven to 200°C/gas mark 6 and fill a muffin tray with paper cases.
- Measure out the dry ingredients into a bowl.
- Add the wet ingredients and mix together. Believe me, a lumpy batter makes better muffins so don't over-mix!
- Spoon mixture into the paper cases and sprinkle the extra choc chips on top.
- Cook for 20 minutes.

Top tips!
Try using white chocolate chips.

Make dinky mini-muffins (these take less time to cook so check on them after 10 minutes).

Cookie Crowns
Any time is cookie time!

150g plain flour
100g soft butter
50g caster sugar

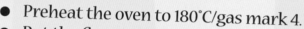

- Preheat the oven to 180°C/gas mark 4.
- Put the flour into a mixing bowl. Rub in the soft butter with your fingertips, then add the sugar and mix to form a stiff dough.
- Roll out the cookie dough to ½ cm thickness.
- Grab your crown cutter and make some shapes!
- Place the crowns in the oven for 6–10 minutes until pale gold.
- Allow to cool on a rack before icing.

Top tip!
There are heaps of cute cookie cutters to choose from. Hunt down: letters of the alphabet (you can spell out your friends' names or a funny message) ● hearts ● Christmas trees ● cats ● stars ● flowers ● lips ● numbers

Top tip!
Remember you can make icing any colour you like!

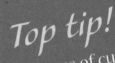

Hey, Cupcake!

What's a princess party without cupcakes?

(Makes 12)

125g butter, softened
125g caster sugar
2 large eggs
125g self-raising flour
½ teaspoon vanilla extract
2–3 tablespoons milk
icing sugar
food colouring and decorations (optional)

- Preheat the over to 180°C/gas mark 4 and fill a muffin tray with paper cases.
- Put all the ingredients except the milk in a food processor and blitz. Add the milk and blitz again until you have a smooth mixture.
- Divide the cupcake into the paper cases.
- Cook for 15–20 minutes.
- Let the cakes cool – then ice.
- Get creative with the decorations!

Top tips!

Have friends over and make and/or decorate the cupcakes together.

To make chocolate cupcakes, take out a tablespoonful of flour and replace with a tablespoonful of cocoa.

Top tips!

Mini-cupcakes are super-cute but the take less time to cook (about 10 minutes).

You can decorate with whatever you like. Try: gold buttons • dolly mixtures • little silver balls • hundreds and thousands

Flapjack Heaven

**Flapjacks are delicious, they keep for days
AND they're good for you. Perfect!**

(Makes about 15 flapjacks)

80g brown sugar
40g butter
60g margarine
250g oats
pinch of salt
1 banana
3 tablespoons honey

- Preheat the oven to 220°C/gas mark 7.
- Melt the butter and the margarine in a deep saucepan over a very low heat.
- Add the brown sugar and 2 tablespoons of honey, and mix well.
- Mix in the oats slowly, stirring all the time.
- Add the salt.
- Mash the banana into a pulp and mix into the oats. It will take a few minutes to make sure the banana is fully mixed in.
- Get a knife and spread the oat mixture evenly over a baking tray.
- Place the baking tray on the middle shelf of the oven and bake for about 15 minutes. The flapjacks are ready when they turn a darker golden brown.

Top tip!
It's easier to cut the flapjack into pieces when it is cool.

Princess in a Panic

continued from page 47

OK, I *know*. I *know* it's stupid to think someone might have stolen my journal with the intention of either publishing it serially in a newspaper or using the information in it to bring down the Genovian throne.

But I knew the thing that has MOST LIKELY happened to my journal – the worst, most horrifying possibility of all (that someone at school has got their hands on it) – wouldn't impress Dad at all.

But the truth is, if this has happened – if someone from school has my journal – the entire population of Albert Einstein High School is going to find out the truth about some things I have been trying *very hard* to keep private.

In which case, my life will be over.

That's all. Just over.

I will have to change schools.

Schools? I will have to change *countries*. I will have to move permanently to Genovia, kiss Manhattan Public Access Cable and H&H Bagels with vegetable cream cheese goodbye forever.

That is the only way I can think of to avoid the cataclysmic event that will result, should the contents of my journal be made public at Albert Einstein High School.

And if that's not a matter of national security, I don't know what is.

Because, seriously, I can just picture Lana Weinberger pulling a total *Cruel Intentions* and standing up on one of the tables in the cafeteria and reading selections from my journal out loud during first-period lunch! Like for instance all the paragraphs dedicated to my frustration over Lana's

constant stream of observations over the years, pertaining to my lack of frontal lobes.

And I don't mean the cranial kind.

And since Lana's a cheerleader and all, you know her voice would carry really far.

But Dad so totally does not get the direness of the situation. I mean, he's never met Lana. He has no idea that she will stop at nothing when it comes to the public humiliation of me!

Princess in a Panic continues on page 66

Sun-kissed Princess

Princess, be super-careful in the sun. Even if you tan easily you are still doing damage to your skin by sunbathing. Remember: pale is pretty, but if you DO want a summer glow, you have to learn how to fake it.

Read the instructions before you start – not all products are the same.

Before you buy fake tan, do some research – ask friends for recommendations and read the 'tried and tested' pages in magazines or on the Internet.

Get scrubbing – fake tan clings to dry skin so exfoliate first.

Get scrubbing – fake tan clings to dry skin so exfoliate first.

Get scrubbing – fake tan clings to dry skin so exfoliate first.

60

Moisturize – then wait two hours before you apply fake tan.

Moisturize – then wait two hours before you apply fake tan.

Colour can transfer on to your clothes so it's best to fake tan at night and wear some baggy old PJs. When you wake up you'll be radiant and bronzed to perfection!

Take a cotton-wool pad and rub your hairline, eyebrows and nails after you finish to get rid of excess product.

Wash your hands afterwards – orange palms are not cool, Princess!

61

Memory Book

Like Princess Mia, you might keep a daily diary.
But it's still fun to keep a 'Book of the Year'.

Throughout the year collect lots of bits and pieces in a shoebox. Things like:

- pictures (photo-booth snaps from a great day/night out with friends – make a note on the back of the date and where you were)
- cuttings from mags
- sayings
- poems
- quotes
- lyrics
- photos
- recipes
- thoughts
- tickets for movies, gigs
- notes from your friends
- bits of fabric
- tube/bus tickets from a special day
- extracts from your diary
- bits of wrapping paper from your birthday or Christmas
- postcards

Allow a double page per memory. You can write as little or as much as you like about each memory. But use the inspirational bits and pieces to decorate the page. If you like drawing, decorate the pages with pictures and doodles.

You can add things to your memory book throughout the year or collect loads of stuff and then spend a whole weekend or school holiday working on it.

Decorate the outside of the notebook with anything you like – gorgeous paper, pictures from magazines, your own drawings, photos . . .

Princess in a Muddle!

1. One of the royal words below ISN'T in the grid. But which one is it...?

PRINCE
CHARMING
CROWN
THRONE
SCEPTRE
DIAMOND
BALLGOWN
PALACE

N	A	P	A	E	F	D	G	E	R	N	N
J	I	M	O	R	U	F	N	W	N	N	H
J	S	P	N	B	L	H	K	E	Z	G	H
D	F	R	M	T	H	R	O	N	E	S	C
O	N	I	I	R	M	H	W	C	T	T	K
P	P	N	R	A	R	O	S	S	E	L	X
A	O	C	G	P	G	N	H	C	P	A	O
L	E	E	G	L	W	X	C	E	U	B	K
A	K	F	L	O	Q	R	N	P	O	A	A
C	H	A	R	M	I	N	G	T	M	R	A
E	B	C	T	F	R	O	U	R	M	F	D
X	R	S	C	T	C	K	H	E	B	I	D

2. Eight letters of the alphabet are missing below. When you've found which ones they are, rearrange them to reveal the name of a popular THE PRINCESS DIARIES character!

B, C, D, G, H, J, K, M, N, P, Q, R, S, V, W, X, Y, Z

64

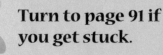
Turn to page 91 if you get stuck.

Holiday Princess Puzzle

Every princess loves the summer holidays!
But these vacation essentials are all mixed up.
Can you solve the anagrams?

LSAGSUSENS

SUNGLASSES

LIPF SLOPF

FLIP-FLOPS

NIBIIK

BIKINI

NASTUN TOILNO

SUNTAN LOTION

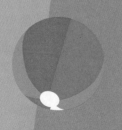

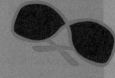

CEAHB WELOT

BEACH TOWEL

The answers are on page 91.

Princess in a Panic

continued from page 59

Instead, my dad just went, all calmly, like he was talking to a mental patient, that Genovia has no enemies and that, even if it did, it was highly unlikely any state secrets would have been revealed in the journal of the teenage daughter of its reigning monarch, and that while it was worrying that the paparazzi might find and publish my fevered scribblings, we would just have to deal with that when it happens, by suing them.

Which doesn't address the fact that my darkest secrets will already be splashed all over the world for the entire planet – and my boyfriend – to read!

Dad went on to suggest that I must have been writing extremely inflammatory things in my journal. Otherwise I wouldn't be worrying so much. So it's probably just as well, he said, that it's gone.

Inflammatory? As if! All I ever write about in my journal is the truth. That's what my mother gave it to me for in the first place: so I'd have a place to express my emotions, since I seem to

have trouble expressing them verbally. What is so inflammatory, I would like to know, about my emotions? What is so inflammatory about the TRUTH???? Isn't the truth supposed to set you free????

But when I think about the convoluted circle of lies my life has become lately, I can't really imagine the truth ever setting me free. All I can see it doing is making my already hellish, practically unbearable life even more intolerable.

I just thought of something. Something even worse than my journal falling into the hands of an enemy of Genovia, or the paparazzi, or even Lana.

What if my best friend Lilly has my journal? And is *reading* it????

Except that if she had, I'm pretty sure I'd have heard about it by now. You know, looking back, I could sort of see how some of the things I might have written about her could be construed in the wrong way, thus making them seem what my father said. You know. Inflammatory.

Princess in a Panic *continues on page 78*

As Easy as 1, 2, 3...

The Princess Diaries book titles are puns on the book number. Can you remember all the titles? (No peeking at your collection!)

The Princess Diaries

The Princess Diaries: Take Two

The Princess Diaries: Third Time Lucky

The Princess Diaries: Mia Goes Fourth

The Princess Diaries: Give Me Five

The Princess Diaries: Six Sational

The Princess Diaries: Seventh Heaven

The Princess Diaries: After Eight

Look out for: The Princess Diaries: To the Nines

What would you call the tenth book in the series? Try out some ideas here:

The Princess Diaries: Tenth Time

The Princess Diaries: Last

The Princess Diaries: Final

You can check your answers on page 92.

Princess in Print

Putting pen to paper is easier than you think. Princess Mia always writes in her diary. So don't be scared and don't listen to anyone who says you can't do it. You can! Make like Mia and get scribbling!

Try writing:
- stories
- poems
- articles for magazines
- plays
- song lyrics
- a diary.

When you're writing a diary, write down your thoughts and feelings about things – don't just write facts about what you did that day.

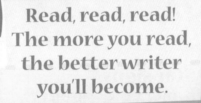

Read, read, read! The more you read, the better writer you'll become.

Write about what YOU care about.

Write in your own style – don't try and copy someone else.

Daydream!

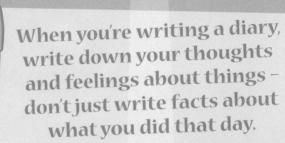

The star signs are grouped into four elements: FIRE, WATER, AIR, EARTH. Find out which element you are and what secrets it reveals about your personality.

WATER
A princess with creative flair

Star signs:
CANCER, PISCES, SCORPIO

Water signs are sensitive and arty – but you can be a bit scatterbrained and indecisive sometimes! You're an amazing friend, who always has time to listen – just make sure you give yourself, and your incredible creativity, enough time and attention.

Pretty in: Turquoise, white, silver

Friends with: Earth signs – they keep your feet on the ground when you're taken away on a wave of wistfulness!

72

FIRE
A princess with passion

Star signs:
ARIES, LEO, SAGITTARIUS

Fire signs can be hot-headed but they're also warm-hearted. You are always honest – a great attribute. Just watch out you don't upset people with your feisty outspokenness. You love being the centre of attention, but people adore being your friend because you're fun-loving and super-generous.

Pretty in: Orange, red, gold

Friends with: Air signs – they fan your fieriness just enough to create the perfect balanced friendship!

Princess

EARTH
A princess with a heart

Star signs:
TAURUS, VIRGO, CAPRICORN

Earth signs always have their feet on the ground and don't like taking too many risks. Just make sure you're not sensible all the time – sometimes it's fun to let go and be a tiny bit spontaneous! You're a caring, supportive friend and everyone knows they can count on you.

Pretty in: Green, yellow, brown

Friends with: Water signs – they make sure your deepest feelings come bubbling to the surface!

AIR
A princess with dreams

Star signs:
GEMINI, LIBRA, AQUARIUS

Air signs are sparky and imaginative – they just love to chat! You're no airhead – but be careful you don't get so carried away by your daydreaming that you forget to listen. Your friends find your unique style inspiring and love hearing all your latest kooky ideas!

Pretty in: Pink, baby blue, purple

Friends with: Fire signs – they can help turn all your weird and wonderful ideas into reality with their flames of enthusiasm!

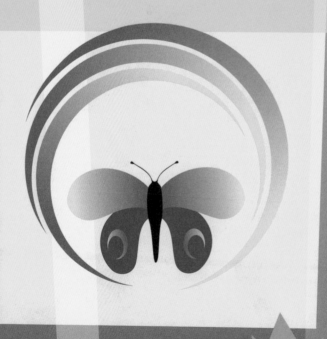

Princess's Personal Style

What is 'personal style'?

Well, it's all about taking inspiration from the things and people around you – without becoming a slave to fashion. Princess Mia doesn't care if Doc Marten boots are fashionable or not – she makes them work for her and they're a key part of her signature look. So find what works for you – and remember: it's cool to be quirky!

Coloured tights can look great – from pillar-box red to neon pink, there's a shade out there for you! To make this look super-funky, try wearing a bright pair of fishnet tights on top of your coloured tights. Don't be afraid to mix and match!

Change the laces
in your trainers
to patterned or
coloured ones.

**Update a boring cardy by
sewing on some quirky
buttons. You can find amazing
buttons in the haberdashery
section of a department store.**

Just because it's
called a necklace you
don't have to wear it
around your neck! Try
wearing chains and
beads as belts . . .

75

Your Crowning Glory

When it comes to hair, there's one bit of advice that applies to all princesses:
Work with what you've got!

OTHER RULES

1.

- Princesses can have curly hair.
- Princesses can have straight hair.
- Princesses can have dark hair, blonde hair, ginger hair or green hair.
- Princesses can have cornrows, extensions, crew cuts or dreadlocks.

2.

If you have curly hair, don't spend forty-five minutes every morning attempting to straighten out all the kinks. Remind yourself that many people spend large amounts of money trying to achieve the waves that you have been blessed with naturally.

3.

If you have straight hair, don't struggle with curling tongs, rollers, etc. They are not necessary! Anyway, they will ultimately defeat you and you will end up frustrated and exhausted. You will start the day in a bad mood.

Of course, it is nice to have a change every now and then, or for special occasions. But you should stick to three simple rules to get hair fit for any young, gorgeous and über-fashionable heir to the throne:

a) A princess's hair must be clean.
b) A princess's hair must not be in her eyes.
c) A princess's hair must not take more than fifteen minutes to style.

Princess in a Panic

continued from page 69

On the other hand, Lilly is exactly the sort of person who *would* steal somebody else's journal and then not say anything. She'd just keep it, and then conduct weird psychological experiments on the person, for her own twisted amusement.

And I could probably count on giant chunks of my journal showing up in some medical journal like *Psychology Today*, under the heading 'An Examination of Neuroses in the Modern Teen', by

Dr Lilly Moscovitz, PhD. All the names and stuff would be changed, but you would totally know it was me. And all these psychiatrists all over America would be talking about me – Patient X – and my obsession with my flat-chestedness and my compulsive nail-biting.

Seriously. I'm expecting it to happen any minute.

Or – oh my God, I didn't even think of this before – what if MICHAEL found my journal?

This would be way, way worse than even the paparazzi or Lana getting their hands on it.

Because THEN MICHAEL WILL KNOW HOW GOOD I THINK HIS NECK SMELLS!

No boy should EVER find out that his girlfriend thinks his neck smells good. That kind of thing can only go straight to a boy's head, making him start to think he doesn't have to take his girlfriend out on proper dates and IM her at regular intervals!

Oh God, this is awful . . .

But wait. Surely if Michael found my journal, he would simply give it back to me. Michael would never violate the holy bond of trust our love has

wrought between us. Michael would never –

ACK! The limo is pulling up in front of the Plaza. I *can't* go upstairs and face a princess lesson – not to mention Grandmere – right now. I'm too busy freaking out over my boyfriend possibly knowing how good I think his neck smells!

THIS CAN'T BE HAPPENING! MICHAEL CANNOT—

Princess in a Panic *continues on page 86*

Princess in Love

Princess Mia offers some essential advice on how to get the prince of your dreams!

Be friendly, but do not come on too strong: smile at the guy and say hi when you see him. If an opportunity for conversation crops up, seize it, but do not go out of your way to make this happen (for instance, don't pretend to bump into him then drop your tiara. Boys can see straight through this; they are not as dumb as they seem).

Look neat and pretty around him. Clearly this is not possible if you have gym together, but try to look as neat and pretty as possible, within reason.

Don't forget to listen – there is nothing more irresistible than a good listener. A good listener:
● never interrupts ● makes eye contact ● lets the person say everything he or she has to say before speaking herself.

Try to keep things light. Don't blurt out all your problems - no matter how interesting or dramatic you might think they are - or talk badly about mutual acquaintances or gossip in a mean way. Remember, you are trying to impress him with your wit and charm, not scare him.

You may need to resort to more drastic measures, such as joining the same club he belongs to or showing up at the same events/gigs/movies he's going to. Just make sure you genuinely do have a few things in common or you'll have nothing to talk about when the two of you finally end up going out.

Don't get upset if you have a lot of conversations with the same guy and he doesn't ask you out. Boys do not mature as rapidly as girls and he may not even be thinking along those lines yet.

If, after all this, the guy still hasn't asked you out, you may need to take the bull by the horns (so to speak) and ask him out yourself!

83

Colour Me Princess

Colour can enhance and change your mood – some colours make you feel happy, some make you feel calm, some make you feel creative.

Your favourite colour says a lot about your personality. Are you a Pink Princess or a Red Princess – and what does that say about you?

RED
Self-confident
Inspirational ● Energetic
You like to be noticed

ORANGE
Party princess ● Chatty ● Smiley
You like to get along
with everyone

YELLOW
Intelligent ● Thoughtful ● Generous
You like to cheer people up

84

GREEN
Relaxed • Down-to-earth
Romantic
You like to be with your friends

PINK
Loyal • Loving • Approachable
You like pretty things

BLUE
Dreamy • Peaceful • Open-minded
You like to keep everyone happy

PURPLE
Creative • Relaxing to be around
You like to chill out

Princess in a Panic

continued from page 81

Tuesday, October 25, 4 p.m., the Plaza

Oh. OK. So it turns out my journal was in Grandmere's bathroom at the Plaza the whole time. She just hurled it at my head as I walked into my princess lesson, telling me the maid found it and thought it was garbage and almost threw it away!!!!

I nearly swallowed my tongue, I was so freaked out. Of all the people I imagined finding my

journal, Grandmere was the only one I DIDN'T think of!

And I've probably written more mean things in this journal about her than anyone else I know!!!!

But when I asked her – with my heart in my throat – if she'd read any of it, Grandmere just rolled her eyes and said she has far more important things to do than read the pathetic ramblings of her teenage granddaughter. Then she told me I ought to keep better track of my belongings, and that real princesses are not careless with their things.

As punishment, she is having me memorize all twenty-four names of the Sultan of Brunei (Kebawah Duli Yang Maha Mulia Paduka Seri Baginda Sultan Haji Hassanal Bolkiah Al-Mu'izzaddin Waddaulah ibni Almarhum Sultan Haji Omar Ali Saifuddien Sa'adul Khairi Waddien).

But I don't care, because I have my journal back!!!! And it did not fall into the hands of any Genovian enemies, the paparazzi, Lana, Lilly or – worse, so much worse – my boyfriend.

YAY!!!!

I think a little prayer of thanks is in order.

Dear God, I know I am not necessarily the nicest person in the world, but I do try, you know, by not eating meat and regularly giving alms to the poor (in the form of my father donating a hundred dollars a day to Greenpeace in my name so long as I do my princess duties, and of course my leaving my recyclable cans and bottles outside by the trash for the homeless to redeem instead of taking them to the grocery store to collect the deposit back myself).

So thank you so much for having mercy on me and NOT letting my boyfriend be the person who found and read my journal (even though I know he is totally not the snooping type. Still, the temptation might have been too strong, even for an upstanding citizen like Michael to resist).

Thank you, God. And in return for this favour, I promise never to write anything mean about anyone in my journal EVER, EVER AGAIN.

I really mean it this time.

I SWEAR!!!!!

Solutions

Page 16

1. ROMANCES 2. VIOLIN
3. GRANDMERE 4. LARS
5. ALGEBRA 6. ROCKY

W	R	O	C	K	Y	N	B	Y	F	D	A
U	V	E	C	H	Y	N	S	W	P	K	L
G	R	A	N	D	M	E	R	E	O	D	G
H	W	B	I	Y	S	K	M	Q	L	Y	E
E	B	A	L	I	Q	B	A	M	X	N	B
A	U	Y	O	S	E	C	N	A	M	O	R
G	Y	S	I	L	A	R	S	Z	R	I	A
K	E	D	V	M	T	P	L	M	Q	X	S

Page 26

Page 27

Page 64

N	A	P	A	E	F	D	G	E	R	N	N
J	I	M	O	R	U	F	N	W	N	F	H
J	S	P	N	B	L	H	K	E	Z	G	M
D	F	R	M	T	H	R	O	N	E	S	C
O	N	I	R	M	H	W	C	T	T	T	K
P	P	N	R	A	R	O	S	S	E	L	X
A	O	C	G	P	G	N	H	C	P	A	O
L	E	E	G	L	W	X	C	E	U	B	K
A	K	F	L	O	Q	R	N	P	O	A	A
C	H	A	R	M	I	N	G	T	M	R	A
E	B	C	T	F	R	O	U	R	M	F	D
X	R	S	C	T	C	K	H	E	B	I	D

1. The missing word is DIAMOND.
2. The character is FAT LOUIE.

Page 65

SUNGLASSES
FLIP-FLOPS
BIKINI
SUNTAN LOTION
BEACH TOWEL

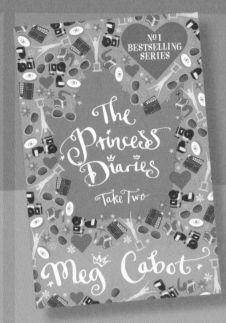

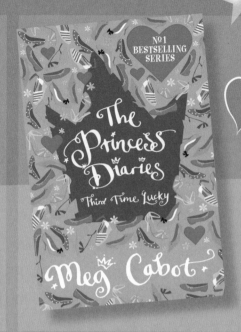

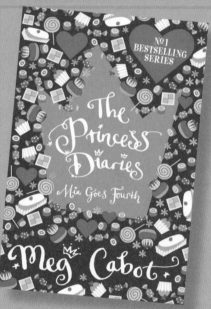

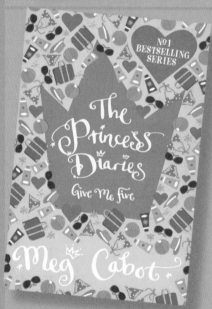

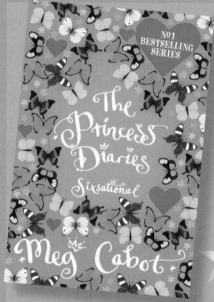

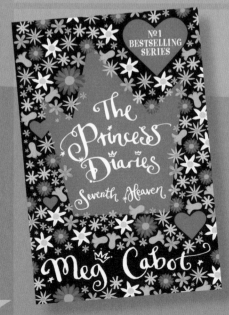

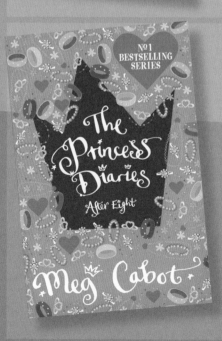

Have you read them all?

Don't miss these other fantastic Meg Cabot books!

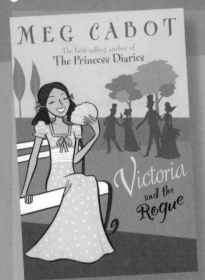

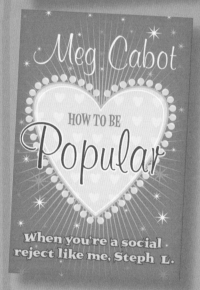

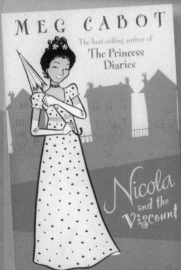